FULL MOON RISING

Joanne Taylor

Illustrated by Susan Tooke

Tundra Books

Published in Canada by Tundra Books,
481 University Avenue, Toronto, Ontario M5G 2E9

Published in the United States by Tundra Books of Northern New York,
P.O. Box 1030, Plattsburgh, New York 12901

Library of Congress Control Number: 2002102985

National Library of Canada Cataloguing in Publication

Taylor, Joanne
     Full moon rising

ISBN 0-88776-548-3

1. Moon – Juvenile literature. I. Tooke, Susan II. Title.

QB582.T39 2002   j523.3   C2002-900772-0

We acknowledge the financial support of the Government of Canada through the Book Publishing Industry Development Program and that of the Government of Ontario through the Ontario Media Development Corporation's Ontario Book Initiative. We further acknowledge the support of the Canada Council for the Arts and the Ontario Arts Council for our publishing program.

Design: Terri Nimmo

Printed in Hong Kong, China

2 3 4 5 6   07 06 05 04 03

To my husband, Robin, and our daughters,
Jeannie and Anna, with great love;
and with deep gratitude to my friend Susan Tooke
JT

For my dear son, Scott Ian Riker.
From each coast, we look at the moon.
ST

Acknowledgments
The illustrator would like to thank The Ross Farm Museum,
David Poole, Jane Buss, and The Writers' Federation of Nova Scotia
for their support and assistance.

January

WOLF MOON

❧

January brings
the Wolf Moon,
the wild Wolf Moon.
Frost has painted pictures
on our windowpanes.
We are cosy indoors.
Out in the snow-white,
moon-white fields,
the wolves howl.
They sing storm songs
to their brother moon.

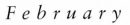

SNOW MOON

❧

Now we are deep in winter,

deep in white,

when the Snow Moon comes

in February.

Pine branches bend lower

with each snowfall.

We keep the feeders full.

It's hard on the animals

and birds in the deep drifts.

This is the hungry time.

SAP MOON

❧

Sap Moon rises in March.
Days thaw and freeze
and thaw again.
We ride out to the sugar bush
to help Mom and Dad
tap the trees and boil the sap
down, down, down
to make maple syrup.
We'll drizzle maple taffy
on the clean snow.
I can almost taste it now,
that snow candy!

GRASS MOON

April is the Grass Moon.

New green covers

dull brown earth.

Trees are waiting, waiting

for their sudden spring leaves.

Lambs are born.

The earth is waking.

Does it dream

in its winter sleep,

like we do?

May

PLANTING MOON

In May, Dad is still plowing
when the Planting Moon
rises each evening.
Mom plants her flower seedlings.
We dig up the vegetable garden.
We're growing our own
patch of pumpkins
to sell in the fall.
We all stop for supper.
Mom has to call Dad in.
Even farmers have to eat.

June

HONEY MOON

June's moon
is the Honey Moon.
We celebrate when
our cousin gets married.
People used to drink mead,
brewed from honey,
at wedding feasts.
But we're having
strawberry punch.
We make a toast
to the bride and groom.
Long life!
Happy life!

July

HAY MOON

~

July brings the Hay Moon.

We all work hard.

Cut hay has dried

in the fields.

The air is still and hot.

But dark clouds carry a warning.

Friends arrive to help us

get the bales in the barn.

Everybody hurries

to finish the work

before the thunderstorms come.

August

CORN MOON

August is so hot, you'd think

the Corn Moon would pop.

We list all the cold words -

ice cream, snowball, popsicle.

It doesn't help us cool off.

Nanny and Papa come out

for our first corn boil.

Fields are full of barley and wheat

and golden corn.

My stomach is full of corn, too.

September

HARVEST MOON

In September, Mom sings
of the Harvest Moon.
Our garden and orchard
are almost empty now.
The kitchen is full!
Mom and Dad
make hundreds of jars
of jams and pickles,
red and yellow and green.
We take our harvest
to the farmers' market.
Our pumpkins are the best.

October

HUNTER MOON

❧

Hunter Moon lights
the sky in October.
We're not allowed
to walk in the woods now.
It's hunting season.
Papa wears an orange vest and cap
to keep him safe.
When he gets home,
we sit on the steps together.
He has Mom's gingersnaps
with his tea.
The air smells of ginger
and winter.

BEAVER MOON

Beaver Moon makes
its home in November.
We hike in the national park.
No hunters allowed here.
Where are the ducks and geese?
They flew south.
Where are the deer,
the porcupines and raccoons?
They are hidden, resting.
Only the beavers are in sight.
They work hard
to build their winter lodge.
Busy as beavers.

LONG-NIGHT MOON

∾

December brings
the Long-Night Moon,
the shortest days,
the longest nights,
the darkest time of year.
What can we do
to cheer us up
in the cold dark time?
We can get ready
for the holidays!
We decorate.
We celebrate
with family and friends.
We are together.
That's how we light up
the dark time
under the Long-Night Moon.

"Once in a Blue Moon"

According to older folklore, when one of the seasons contains four full moons, the third is called a Blue Moon. In quite recent folklore, a Blue Moon is the second full moon in any calendar month. On average, that happens once every two-and-a-half years. The third version refers to the rare times when the moon appears blue, whether it's full or not.

In any case, "once in a Blue Moon" has come to mean "not often."

Is the moon really ever blue? The moon doesn't actually change color, but it appears to do so if there are a lot of volcanic-dust or forest-fire particles in the air. When the Indonesian volcano, Krakatau, exploded in 1883, sunsets around the world were brilliantly colored for several years and the moon appeared blue.

Did you ever hear of a Black Moon?

I f there is no full moon in a month, it's sometimes called a Black Moon. February is so short that, in years where two other months - usually January and March - each have double full moons, there isn't time for a full moon in February. This happens, on average, about three times each century.

FULL MOON NAMES

Throughout the world, people of many cultures have named the full moons. These names reflected the climate and seasonal activities. The following is a list of names that were frequently used.

JANUARY
Wolf, Storm, Old, Ice, Moon After Yule, Cold,
Big Water Ice

FEBRUARY
Snow, Hunger, Opening Buds, Ice in River is Gone, Bony

MARCH
Sap, Maple Sugar, Worm, Crow, Crust, Death,
Lenten, Seed, Windy

APRIL
Grass, Awakening, Pink, Egg, Fish, Seed, Frog,
Red Grass Appearing, Hare, Rain

MAY
Planting, Flower, Corn Planting, Milk, Budding,
Dyad, Idle

JUNE
Honey, Strawberry, Rose, Hot, Mead, Green Corn

JULY
Hay, Thunder, Buck, Wort, Bellowing Buffalo, Ripe Corn

AUGUST
Corn, Grain, Sturgeon, Red, Dog Days, Barley, Ripe

SEPTEMBER
Harvest*, Fruit, Dying Grass,
Nut, Elk Call

OCTOBER
Hunter, Leaf Falling, Harvest*, Travel, Blood,
Big Wind, Yellow Leaf, Big Feast

NOVEMBER
Beaver, Geese Going, Frost, Tree, Trading,
Owl, Ice Forming

DECEMBER
Long-Night, Cold, Oak, Moon Before Yule,
Big Freezing, Popping Trees

*Each year the full moon that falls closest to the
Autumnal Equinox (the first day of autumn) gets
the name Harvest Moon.